Cont

Tom   Joey

CHAPTER 1

Tennis Tactics

The Wimbledon Tennis Championships are played once a year. To win the title of best player takes a lot of really hard training. So Tom and Joey have been training really hard! Every afternoon after school they go to the park and practise their tennis. They want to make sure that they are ready to play in this year's Wimbledon championships.

Tom arrives at Joey's place, ready
to go to the park.

Tom "Are you ready to go?"
Joey "I have to have something to
    eat, then I'll be ready."

Tom "You're always eating."

Joey "That's because I'm always hungry."

Tom "You might have a big worm living in your stomach."

Joey "No, I haven't. I'm just growing fast."

Tom "Maybe, but if you keep eating as much as you do, you might just end up growing out not up."

Joey "Well, I've finished eating now, so are you ready to go?"

Tom "I've been ready since I got here."

Joey collects his tennis racquet and together the boys walk to the park.

CHAPTER 2

The Tennis Court

In the middle of the park is a basketball court. A large brick wall runs down the side of the court. The wall has a line painted across it, the same height as a tennis net.

Tom "So are we going to play singles or doubles?"

Joey "Well, I want to be Lleyton Hewitt—he always wins."

Tom "Okay. I'll be Tim Henman— *Tiger Tim!*"

Joey "Well, if that's who you're going to be, then we should play doubles."

Tom "Why?"

Joey "Because he never wins. He comes second every time when he plays me."

Tom "If he played *you* all the time he'd *always* win."

Joey "No, I'm Lleyton Hewitt so he never wins against me."

Tom reaches into his pocket and
pulls out a piece of rag.

Joey "What are you goin' to do with
that?"
Tom "Good players always wear a
headband."

Joey "Yeah, but great players like Lleyton wear their hat back to front."

Joey turns his hat around, like Lleyton's. Tom ties on his headband, then tightens it a bit.

Tom holds his tennis racquet like a guitar.

Tom "You know the best thing about having a tennis racquet?"

Joey "You can play tennis with it."

Tom "Yeah! But when you're not playing tennis, you can use the racquet as a guitar."

Joey "Well, after losing against me, you'll want to start playing the guitar."

Tom "Let's start playing and see who's really the loser."

CHAPTER 3

Warm-up

Tom and Joey start hitting the ball against the brick wall. Tom hits first. The ball bounces back and Joey takes the next hit.

Joey "Are we playing singles or doubles?"

Tom "I reckon we should play doubles."

Joey "Cool. Let's play then."

Lleyton and Tim are best mates and they really like playing together.

Tom "So who are we going to play against?"

Joey "I don't care. Let's play some young unknown players."

Tom "Yeah, we should be able to beat them."

Joey "So you will have to give them names."

Tom "Why don't we just call them 'Silver'?"

Joey "Why Silver?"

Tom "Well, that's what you get when you come second."

Tom hits the ball hard into the brick wall. This time the ball flies back and Joey belts it. The warm-up is complete and the match can begin.

CHAPTER 4

Let the Match Begin

Tom decides that he is the on-court
announcer and it's time to introduce
the players.

Tom *"Ladies and gentlemen. Today's game on centre court stars two great players, Tim Henman and Lleyton Hewitt. Their opponents today are two young challengers. Their names are Cement Silver and Concrete Silver. The challengers are not up to the standard of Henman and Hewitt. They have no hope of winning. The best they can expect to come is second."*

Tom "So who's going to serve first?"

Joey "I will. I've got the best serve."

Tom "Your serve's not better than mine."

Joey "Well, let's say that we both have the best serves in the world."

Tom *"Tim serves the ball. Cement returns the ball. Lleyton belts the ball back at Concrete. The ball hits the edge of Concrete's racquet and goes out of court."*

Joey gives Tom a high-five.

Joey "Great serve, Tim!"

Tom "And a great return, Lleyton!"

Joey "Yeah, we're the best team in the world. Nobody can beat us."

Tom "Look how quiet Cement and Concrete are. They know we're brilliant and are too scared to speak."

Joey "If we keep playing like this they'll never win a point."

Tom "It could be the first time in history that two great players have never lost a point in a game of tennis."

Tom serves again.

Joey *"Another great forehand by Hewitt."*

Tom "And that was another great backhand by me."

Joey *"Hewitt runs really fast across the court. He's so fast and yes, he does another great shot!"*

Tom "Yes, yours was great, but not as good as the one I'm about to do."

Joey "Well this time I'm going to do a two-handed, backhand cross-court power shot. They will never get this back."

"The young pair of Cement and Concrete still haven't said a word, but they keep getting the ball back into play."

Tom "The harder we hit the ball at them, the harder they hit it back at us."

Joey "I've got just the shot that'll beat them."

Tom "So what's that?"

Joey "Watch this!"

Joey runs towards the ball and hits it high in the air.

Tom "What sort of shot is that?"

Joey "It's a lob shot. They'll never be able to get that back."

Tom "That shot's wicked. We've found their weakness."

Joey "The young players won't be able to return the ball."

CHAPTER 5

We Are the Champions

Tom and Joey are beating the young
challengers. They are only one point
away from winning the Wimbledon
championship.

Tom "We only need one more point to win."

Joey "We're the best team in the world."

Tom "I hit the ball straight down the centre of the court."

Joey "But they've hit it back. It's up to me. I'll try the lob shot."

The ball floats over the top of the brick wall. The boys throw their racquets up in the air.

Joey "We've won! We're the champions!"

Tom "That was easy. Cement and Concrete might be good at home, but they are not much good when they play us."

Joey "I reckon we could beat anyone in the world."

Tom "Yeah, I reckon that we're the best in the universe."

Joey "Hey, see that dog running across the park?"

Tom "Yeah."

Joey "He's got our tennis ball in his mouth."

Tom "We'd better chase after him for the ball."

Joey "I can run faster than you."

Tom "Here we go again!"

Tom

Tennis Lingo

Joey

ace When you serve the ball and the player you have served the ball to cannot hit it back.

doubles When two players play together as a team.

lob When you hit the ball really high into the air.

net This runs across the centre of the court. You have to hit the ball over the net.

singles When one tennis player plays against another tennis player.

BOYS RULE!

Tennis Must-dos

☞ Make sure that the brick wall you are playing against is made of smooth bricks.

☞ If you want to be just like Lleyton Hewitt, make sure that you turn your cap back to front.

☞ If you think that you want to be like Andre Agassi then wear really baggy shorts and shave your head.

☞ Learn to play forehand shots as well as backhand shots.

☞ Remember the harder you hit the ball against the brick wall, the faster the ball will come back at you.

☞ Don't throw your racquet when you play a bad shot.

☞ Try to wear really cool-looking clothes.

☞ When you are playing, pretend that you are at the Wimbledon championship and playing on centre court.

☞ If you start to get bored, turn the racquet around and pretend that you are playing a guitar.

Tennis Instant Info

 Pete Sampras has won Wimbledon the most times—7.

Boris Becker is the youngest player to win the Wimbledon singles title. He was 17 years old.

The longest rally (not in a tournament) is one that lasted 17 062 strokes. The rally lasted 9 hours and 6 minutes.

You serve a fault if you serve the ball outside the service lines marked on the court.

A deuce is when the scores in a game are even at three points each.

A ball boy can also be a girl and is the person who collects the balls between points.

In tennis the word "love" means zero. It's used to show that a person hasn't scored a point.

Think Tank

1 What is an ace?

2 How many players are there in a doubles game of tennis?

3 What is a fault?

4 What country does Tim Henman come from?

5 What is a serve?

6 When the umpire calls "let", what has happened?

7 In which country is Wimbledon held?

8 What is a foot fault?

Answers

8 A foot fault is when the player's foot is over the baseline while they are serving.

7 The Wimbledon championship is held in England.

6 "Let" means that the ball you serve touches the top of the net before falling into the serving court.

5 A serve is when the player hits the ball into a certain area of the court to start the game.

4 Tim Henman comes from England.

3 A fault is when the ball being served lands outside the serving court.

2 There are four players in a game of doubles.

1 An ace is when the ball is served so that the player receiving it cannot hit it back.

How did you score?

- If you got all 8 answers correct, then you might be ready to be a professional tennis player.

- If you got 6 answers correct, you need a little more coaching.

- If you got only 4 answers correct, then keep practising against the brick wall.

Felice → ← Phil

Hi Guys!

We have loads of fun reading and want you to, too. We both believe that being a good reader is really important and so cool.

Try out our suggestions to help you have fun as you read.

At school, why don't you use "Tennis Ace" as a play and you and your friends can be the actors. Set the scene for your play. Maybe you can take your tennis racquet to school or maybe you can just use your imagination to pretend that you are on centre court at Wimbledon.

So ... have you decided who is going to be Tom and who is going to be Joey? Now, with your friends, read and act out our story in front of the class.

We have a lot of fun when we go to schools and read our stories. After we finish the kids all clap really loudly. When you've finished your play your classmates will do the same. Just remember to look out of the window— there might be a talent scout from a television station watching you!

Reading at home is really important and a lot of fun as well.

Take our books home and get someone in your family to read them with you. Maybe they can take on a part in the story.

Remember, reading is a whole lot of fun.

So, as the frog in the local pond would say, Read-it!

And remember, Boys Rule!

BOYS RULE!

When We Were Kids

Felice

Phil

Felice "What sort of juice did you think they meant in tennis when you were a kid? Apple? Cranberry? Orange?"

Phil "It's *deuce*, not *juice*, you goof!"

Felice "Yeah, I know. I was just joking."

Phil "Well I'm thirsty. I think I might go and have a glass of deuce."

Felice "Don't you mean *juice*?"

Phil "Yeah, orange deuce."

Felice "How did you ever play tennis when you were a kid if you don't know the difference between *deuce* and *juice*?"

Phil "That's just it—I didn't!"

BOYS RULE!

What a Laugh!

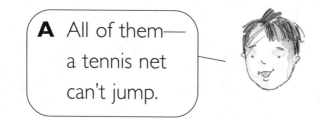

Q Which tennis player can jump higher than the net?

A All of them— a tennis net can't jump.

BOYS RULE!

BOYS RULE! Gone Fishing
Gone Fishing

BOYS RULE! The Tree House
The Tree House

BOYS RULE! Golf Legends
Golf Legends

BOYS RULE! Camping Out
Camping Out

BOYS RULE! Bike Daredevils
Bike Daredevils

BOYS RULE! Water Rats
Water Rats

BOYS RULE! Skateboard Dudes
Skateboard Dudes

BOYS RULE! Tennis Ace
Tennis Ace

BOYS RULE! Basketball Buddies
Basketball Buddies

BOYS RULE! Secret Agent Heroes
Secret Agent Heroes

BOYS RULE! Wet World
Wet World

BOYS RULE! Rock Star
Rock Star

BOYS RULE! Pirate Attack
Pirate Attack

BOYS RULE! Olympic Champions
Olympic Champions

BOYS RULE! Race Car Dreamers
Race Car Dreamers

BOYS RULE! Hit the Beach
Hit the Beach

BOYS RULE! Rotten School Day
Rotten School Day

BOYS RULE! Halloween Gotcha!
Halloween Gotcha!

BOYS RULE! Battle of the Games
Battle of the Games

BOYS RULE! On the Farm
On the Farm